How Your Body Works

Anita Ganeri
Illustrated by Marijan Ramljak

pinwheel

Contents

4 Body bits
Cells are the tiny building blocks of your body.

6 Surface cover
Your skin covers the whole surface of your body.

8 Scaffolding
Your body is supported by your skeleton.

10 Muscle power
Muscles make your body move.

12 Control centre
Your brain controls what your body does.

14 Lookout system
Your senses tell you about the world.

16 Power station
Your lungs give oxygen to your blood.

In one day, you shed 10 billion skin flakes.

A grown-up has 206 bones in his or her body.

The biggest muscle in your body is in your bottom.

You blink 22 times a minute when talking to someone, but only 10 times a minute when you read.

18 Pumping station
Your heart pumps blood around your body.

20 Transport system
Your blood carries food to your body cells.

22 Teeth and chewing
Your teeth chop up and chew your food.

24 Food processing
Your stomach and intestines break down your food.

26 Cleansing department
Your liver cleans up your blood.

28 Waterworks
Your kidneys get rid of waste water.

30 Glossary

32 Index

Your heart beats 4,500 times in one hour.

Your blood has the same amount of salt in it as sea water.

The journey of food through your intestines takes a whole 24 hours!

Your kidneys make 1.5 litres of waste water every day.

Body bits

Your whole body is made up of tiny building blocks called cells. About 50 million cells make you up!

Where are they?

Cells make up every single bit of your body. They make up your bones, brain, nerves, muscles, skin, blood and so on.

Nerve cell

Skin cell

What do they do?

Groups of the same type of cell make up your body tissue, like muscle tissue and skin tissue. Other cells carry messages around your body or fight off germs.

Here are four types of cells – this is what they look like under a microscope.

What do they look like?

Cells come in many different shapes. For example, red blood cells are shaped like tiny doughnuts. Each type of cell has a different job to do.

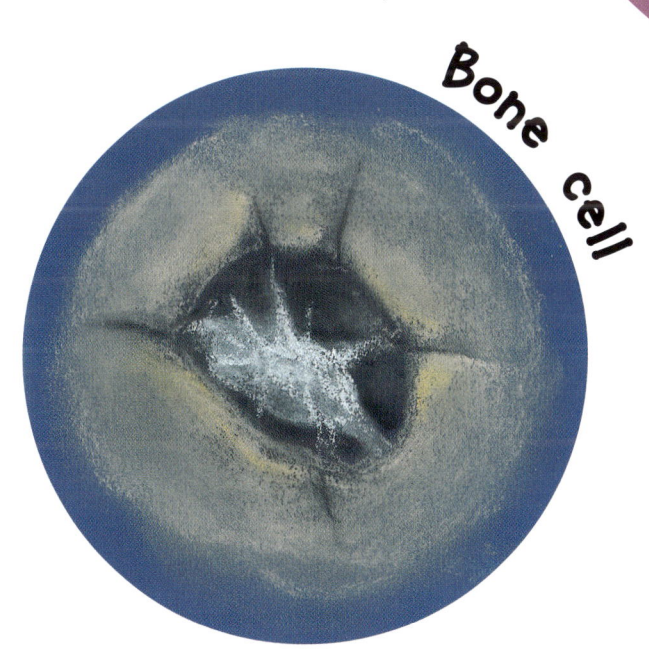

Hair cell

Bone cell

What are they made of?

Each cell is made of about two-thirds water. Inside is a nucleus. The nucleus tells the cell how to work and keeps it alive.

Try this

Look at cell sizes

Most cells are too small to see except under a microscope. The biggest cells are female egg cells. The smallest cells are in your brain. They are just 0.005 mm (0.0002 in) across. See how many dots you can make on this full stop. Hundreds of brain cells would fit on it.

5

Surface cover

Like an enormous bag, your skin holds your body together. It also protects your body from damage, germs and drying out.

Where is it?
Your skin covers the outside of your body from the soles of your feet to your eyelids to your fingertips.

What does it look like?
Skin is soft and stretchy. It can be different colours from pale pink to dark brown. Most of your skin is covered in fine hairs.

What does it do?
Your skin is tough and waterproof to protect your body from harm. It also helps to keep you warm or cool, and allows you to touch and feel things.

How does it work?
When you're cold, you get bumps on your skin called goose bumps. These are made by the hairs on your arms standing on end to keep you warm. When you're hot, sweat trickles from your skin to cool you down.

When you are hot, drops of sweat appear on your skin.

The skin

What is it made of?
Your skin has two layers. The top layer is made of tough, dead cells. The bottom layer is packed with sweat and oil glands, hair follicles and nerve endings.

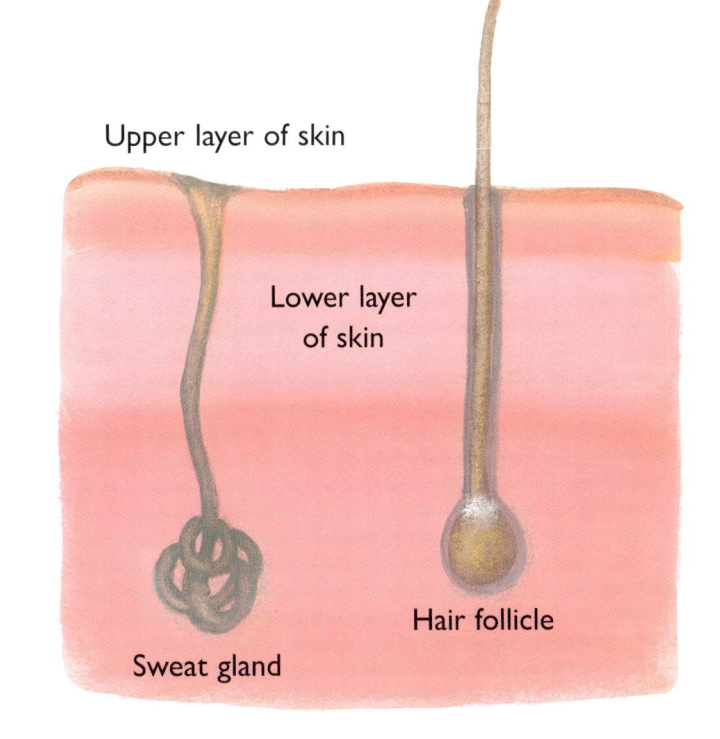

Upper layer of skin

Lower layer of skin

Sweat gland

Hair follicle

When you are cold, goose bumps appear on your skin.

Try this

Make a fingerprint
Press your fingertips firmly down on the ink pad. Then press down on a piece of paper to leave your fingerprints. These are patterns made by tiny ridges on the skin on your fingertips. They help your fingers to grip better. No two people ever have the same fingerprints.

Scaffolding

Your skeleton is like scaffolding inside your body. It stops your body from losing its shape and flopping in a heap.

What is it made of?

Your skeleton is made up of more than 200 bones, joined together. Bones are light so that you can move but are very strong and tough.

What do they look like?

Bones are different shapes and sizes depending on the job they do. For example, your leg bones are long and strong to hold your weight as you walk.

Where are they?

Your bones are inside your body, underneath your skin. Press down on your fingers. Can you feel your hard, knobbly finger bones?

What do they do?

Your skeleton and bones support your body and stop it from collapsing. They also help you to move and protect delicate parts of your body.

Try this

Measure your thighbones

To find the longest bones in your body, measure your legs from the tops to your knees. The bones inside are your thighbones. Your smallest bones are deep inside your ears so you won't be able to measure those!

How do they work?

When you want to move a part of your body, your brain sends a message to your muscles. It tells the muscle to squeeze and get shorter. As the muscle squeezes, it pulls on a bone and makes it move.

This is your body on the outside. Lift the flap to see your muscles underneath.

Control centre

Your brain is your body's control centre. It controls everything that your body does, feels, learns and thinks.

Where is it?
Your brain sits inside the top of your head where it is protected from damage by your skull bones. It is about half the size of your head.

How does it work?
Your brain is connected to every part of your body by wire-like nerves. Nerves carry messages from your body to your brain and from your brain to your body.

What does it look like?
Your brain looks like a soft, pale grey lump. It is wrinkly on the outside and is filled with fluid.

What is it made of?
Your brain is made up of some 10 million nerve cells. They join up to form a vast network for sending signals around your body.

Try this

Watch your brain grow
Like the rest of the body, the brain is mostly water. Put the brain in a bowl of water and watch it grow as it soaks the water up. This will take a few days. Then, take it out of the water and watch it shrink back again.

The brain

What does it do?
The biggest part of your brain is divided into two halves. Each half controls different skills and abilities. The left side controls creative skills and feelings. The right side deals with problem solving and logic.

This is your head on the outside. Lift the flap to see how your brain fits inside.

13

Lookout system

You have five senses – sight, hearing, touch, taste and smell. They tell you what is happening in the outside world.

What are they?
You have five sense organs – your lookout system. You see with your eyes, smell with your nose, hear with your ears, taste with your tongue and touch with your skin.

Where are they?
Your eyes, ears and nose are in your head where they can look out over the outside world. Your tongue is in your mouth so that it can taste your food. Your skin is all over your body.

Try this

Seeing with two eyes
Your eyes are ball-shaped like the bouncy eyeball. Having two eyes is very useful. It gives you a better all-around picture of things. Try shutting one of your eyes, then the other. Can you notice the difference in what you can see?

The eyes

What do they look like?
Your eyes are two jelly-filled balls protected by socket holes in your skull. The coloured part of your eye is your iris. The black dot in the middle is really a hole called the pupil.

White of eye
Pupil
Iris

What do they do?
Your eyes collect light, which bounces off objects and then turns the light into pictures that you can see.

How do they work?
Light enters your eye through the pupil. Behind the pupil is a clear disc called a lens. It bends the light to make an upside-down picture on the back of your eye (the retina). Nerves send signals to your brain. Your brain turns the picture the right way up.

Power station

When you breathe in, your lungs pull oxygen into your body. From your lungs, the oxygen seeps into your blood.

Where are they?
Your two lungs are in your chest where they are protected by your ribs. Your ribs move as you breathe in and out.

What do they look like?
Your lungs are like two squishy bags. When you breathe in, they stretch and fill with air. When you breathe out, they squeeze stale air out.

What are they made of?
Each lung is filled with branching air tubes. At the ends of the tubes are bunches of tiny air sacs, called alveoli. These fill up with air like tiny balloons.

What do they do?
Your lungs help you breathe in oxygen. The oxygen mixes with digested food to give you energy. Your body uses energy from food as fuel to make it work.

Try this

See how your lungs fill with air
Put a little water in a bowl and put the sponge in the bowl. See how it soaks the water up. Your lungs pull in air just as the sponge pulls in water. Now squeeze the sponge to push the water out again.

The lungs

How do they work?
When you breathe in, oxygen goes into your lungs. There, it seeps through the air sac walls into your blood. Your blood carries it around your body where it mixes with food. Waste gas flows the other way. Your blood carries it to your lungs to be breathed out.

Pumping station

Your heart is your body's pumping station. It pumps blood around your body all the time, day and night.

Where is it?
Your heart sits in the middle of your chest, between your two lungs. It is about the size of your clenched fist.

What is it made of?
Your heart is made of a strong muscle, called cardiac muscle, which never tires or stops working (until you die).

What does it do?
Your heart pumps blood around your body because blood carries food and oxygen to all your body cells. Your cells need food and oxygen to work.

What does it look like?
Inside, your heart is divided into four parts called chambers with walls of muscle in between. Tubes called veins and arteries carry the blood in and out of your heart.

Try this

See how your heart pumps
Fill the red balloon with water and fix it to the end of the red plastic tube. Now squeeze the balloon to pump the water along the tube. This is what your heart does when it pumps blood through an artery. Use the blue balloon and blue tube to pump stale blood from around your body back to your heart.

The heart

How does it work?
Blood, without oxygen, flows into the right side of your heart and is pumped to your lungs to pick up oxygen. Then it flows into the left side of your heart where it is pumped to the rest of your body. Each pump is called a heartbeat.

This is your heart on the outside. Lift the flap to see how it works inside.

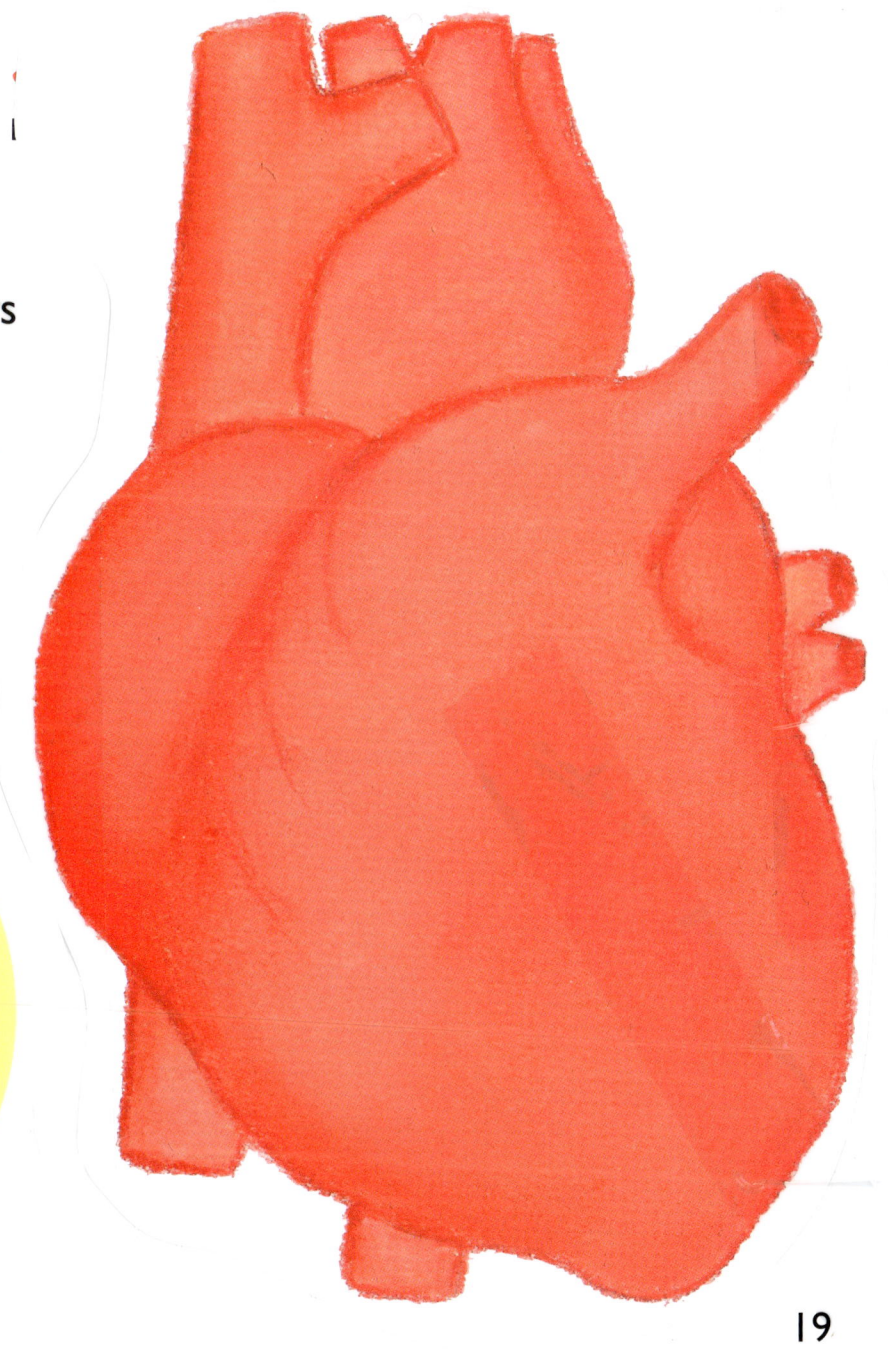

Transport system

Your blood is your body's transport system. It carries food and oxygen to every part of your body, and collects waste.

Where is it?
Your blood flows around through tiny tubes called blood vessels. The three types of blood vessel are arteries, veins and capillaries.

What is it made of?
Blood is made of red and white blood cells and tiny bits of cells called platelets. These cells float in a watery liquid called plasma.

What does it look like?
Blood looks bright red when it is full of oxygen. When the oxygen has been used up, your blood looks purplish-red.

What does it do?
The main job of your blood is to carry oxygen and food around your body. Your body needs these to work. Your blood also collects waste from your cells so that you can get rid of it.

Try this

See how fat sticks to your arteries
Pour some gloop into the red plastic tube and watch how it sticks to the sides. If you eat too much fatty food, the fat may stick to your arteries and stop your transport system from working.

How does it work?

Your heart pumps blood around your body through your blood vessels. Arteries are blood vessels that carry blood away from your heart. Veins are blood vessels that carry blood back to your heart. Your heart keeps your blood moving.

This is your body on the outside. Lift the flap to see how your blood flows around inside.

Teeth and chewing

When you take a bite of food, where does it go next? You grip the food with your lips, then use your teeth to chop and chew it.

Where are they?
Inside your mouth, your teeth are fixed into your jaw bones by long plugs called roots. Over the jaw bones are fleshy gums.

What are they made of?
The outer part of a tooth is made of very strong, white enamel. The softer bits inside a tooth contain tiny blood vessels and nerves.

What do they look like?
Your front teeth are sharp for biting and cutting your food into chunks. Your back teeth are flat and grooved for crushing and grinding your food as you chew.

What do they do?
Your teeth chop and chew your food. They break it into pieces that are small enough for you to swallow.

Enamel

Root

How do they work?

As you chew your food, it gets mixed with saliva, which helps to break it up. Then your tongue rolls the chewed-up food into a ball. It pushes the ball to the back of your throat for you to swallow.

How to have healthy teeth
You need to clean your teeth well to keep them healthy. Try setting a timer, especially at night, to make sure that you brush for a full two minutes. If bits of food get stuck on your teeth, they can cause your teeth to go bad.

Try this

Food processing

Your stomach and intestines are your body's food processors. They work at digesting your chewed-up food.

The stomach

How does it work?

When you swallow, your chewed-up food goes down a tube into your stomach. Your stomach is a thick bag of muscle. Here, your food is mashed and mixed with stomach juices until it becomes something like thick, gloopy soup. After about three hours, a muscle opens at the end of your stomach and the soup flows out.

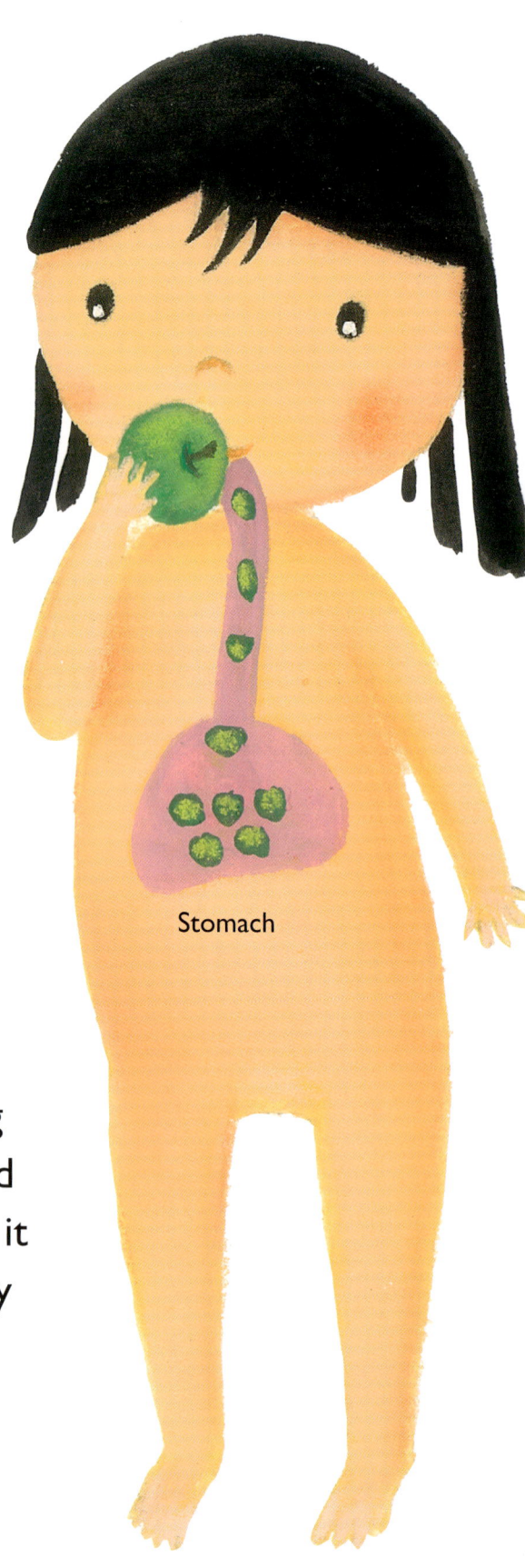

Stomach

Cleansing department

Your liver is vital for keeping your body healthy. It cleans your blood by getting rid of poisons that could make you ill.

Where is it?

Your liver sits near the top of your abdomen, above your stomach and intestines.

This is your body on the outside. Lift the flap to see how your liver fits inside.

Where are the intestines?

From your stomach, your food goes into your intestines. They reach from the lower end of your stomach all the way to your bottom.

What do they look like?

Your intestines are a very long tube, coiled up inside your body. They are divided into your small and your large intestines. Your 'small' intestine is as long as a bus!

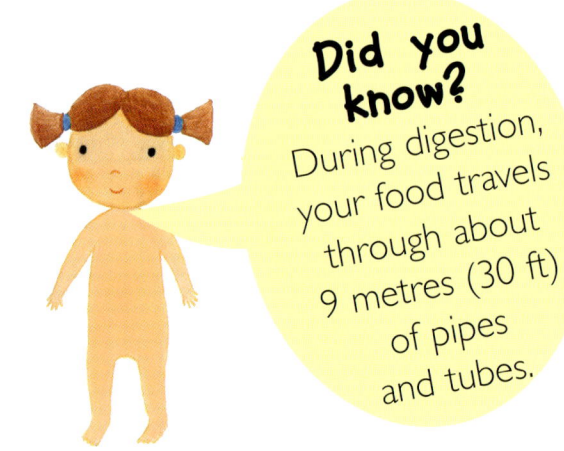

See how food moves along

Put the ball in the plastic 'intestine' casing and push it down the intestine by squeezing the intestine behind it. This is how muscles in your intestines push food along your digestive tube.

Try this

What are they made of?

Your small intestine is lined with millions of tiny bumps called villi. Digested food seeps through the bumps' walls and into your blood.

What do they do?

In your small intestine, food goes into your blood. Water and waste food go into your large intestine. Water seeps through the intestine walls into your blood. Waste food is pushed out of the end of the tube when you go to the toilet.

Did you know?

During digestion, your food travels through about 9 metres (30 ft) of pipes and tubes.

See how big your liver is

Using some kitchen scales, weigh out 1.5 kg (3 lb) of potatoes. That's how much your liver weighs! It's about 20 cm (8 in) wide and 12 cm (4½ in) thick. About 1.5 litres (3 pints) of blood reaches your liver every minute.

Try this

What does it look like?

Your liver is divided into two parts, called the left lobe and right lobe. Large blood vessels carry blood to and from your liver for processing.

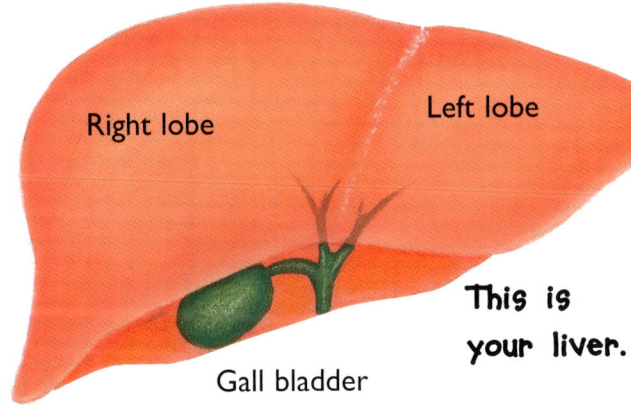

What is it made of?

Each lobe contains thousands of tiny lobules, which are made up of liver cells. A lobule is roughly six-sided in shape. Tiny blood vessels branch off the larger ones and run through each of the lobules.

What does it do?

Apart from cleaning your blood, your liver also helps you to digest your food. Blood from your small intestine carries digested food to your liver. Here, some of the chemicals are stored and some are changed into more useful forms. Your gall bladder is tucked behind your liver. It stores a green liquid called bile, which your liver makes. Bile helps to break down fats in your food.

Right lobe
Left lobe
Gall bladder
This is your liver.

Waterworks

Your two kidneys filter waste water from your blood and turn it into urine. The urine flows out when you go to the toilet.

Where are they?
Your kidneys are in the lower part of your body, just below your ribs. You have one kidney on each side of your body.

What do they look like?
Your kidneys look like two giant red beans. They are about 10 cm (4 in) long and about 4 cm (1½ in) wide. Each one is covered in a thin 'skin'.

What are they made of?
Inside your kidneys are millions of tiny filters called nephrons. Blood vessels carry blood to the filters to be processed.

What do they do?
Blood flows into your kidneys. The kidneys filter out any water that your body does not need, together with other kinds of waste. They turn it into a liquid called urine.

Try this

See how your kidneys filter water

Put the filter paper inside the funnel and stand it in a jug or jar. Pour a little muddy water into the funnel. See how the water filters through, leaving the mud behind. It will drip through very slowly. The filters inside your kidneys work in a similar way.

The kidneys

How do they work?

From your kidneys, the urine is squeezed down two tubes into a stretchy bag called your bladder. When your bladder is full, you need to go to the toilet. Then, the urine flows out of your body through another tube.

Glossary

Abdomen
The middle part of your body between your chest and your pelvis (hips).

Arteries
Arteries are blood vessels that carry oxygen-rich blood from your heart around your body.

Capillaries
Capillaries are tiny blood vessels that branch off from your arteries. The branches join up again to form veins.

Digestion
Your body has to break food down into pieces that are tiny enough to seep into your blood. This is called digestion.

Enamel
A very hard, white material that covers the outside of your teeth.

Glands
Parts of your body, which make different kinds of fluids, such as the sweat and oil glands in your skin.

Hair follicles
Tiny, deep pits all over your body in your skin. Your hair grows out of them.

Nucleus
The part of a cell that carries instructions telling the cell how to work.

Organs
Organs are groups of tissues that work together. Your sense organs are your eyes, nose, ears, tongue and skin.

Oxygen
A gas with no taste or smell. You take in oxygen when you breathe in. Your body cells need oxygen to work.

Saliva
A liquid you make in your mouth that helps you to chew, taste and digest your food.

Sweat
A salty liquid made deep inside your skin. It oozes to the surface through tiny holes to help to cool your body down.

Tissue
Groups of cells working together. Types of body tissue include your skin, muscle, blood, bone and nerve tissue.

Urine
The liquid made by your kidneys, which flows out of your body when you go to the toilet.

Veins
Veins are blood vessels that carry stale blood from your body back to your heart.

Index

A
abdomen 26, 30
arteries 18, 20, 21, 30

B
blood 4, 5, 16, 17, 18, 19, 20–21, 25, 26, 27, 28, 31
blood vessels 20, 21, 22, 27, 28, 30
bones 4, 5, 8, 9, 10, 11, 12, 22, 31
brain 4, 5, 11, 12–13, 15

C
capillaries 20, 30
cells 4–5, 7, 12, 18, 20, 27, 30, 31

E
ears 8, 10, 14, 31
eyes 10, 14, 15, 31

G
gall bladder 27
glands 7, 30

H
hair 5, 6, 7, 30
heart 10, 18–19, 21, 30, 31

I
intestines 24–25, 26, 27

J
joints 9

K
kidneys 28–29, 31

L
liver 26–27
lungs 16–17, 18, 19

M
muscles 4, 10–11, 18, 24, 25, 31

N
nerves 4, 7, 12, 15, 22, 31
nose 14, 31

O
organs 14, 31
oxygen 16, 17, 18, 19, 20, 30, 31

S
senses 14–15, 31
skeleton 8–9
skin 4, 6–7, 8, 10, 14, 30, 31
skull 9, 12, 15
stomach 24–25, 26

T
teeth 22–23, 30
tongue 14, 23, 31

V
veins 18, 20, 21, 30, 31

This is a Pinwheel Book
Created by Pinwheel, a Division of Alligator Books Ltd, Gadd House, Arcadia Avenue, London N3 2JU, UK

Copyright © 2008 Alligator Books Ltd

Author: Anita Ganeri • Illustrator: Marijan Ramljak

All rights reserved. No part of this publication may be reproduced, stored in a retrieval system, or transmitted in any form or by any means electronic, mechanical, photocopying, recording, or otherwise, without the permission of the copyright holder.

ISBN: 978-1-86199-198-0

10 9 8 7 6 5 4 3 2 1

Printed in China